A Splash of Magic

SUE BENTLEY

illustrated by Angela Swan

Grosset & Dunlap
An Imprint of Penguin Group (USA) Inc.

To all the pet bunnies I've met.

Thanks for the hugs!—SB

GROSSET & DUNLAP
Published by the Penguin Group
Penguin Group (USA) Inc., 375 Hudson Street, New York, New York 10014, USA
Penguin Group (Canada), 90 Eglinton Avenue East, Suite 700, Toronto, Ontario M4P 2Y3, Canada
(a division of Pearson Penguin Canada Inc.)
Penguin Books Ltd., 80 Strand, London WC2R 0RL, England
Penguin Group Ireland, 25 St. Stephen's Green, Dublin 2, Ireland (a division of Penguin Books Ltd.)
Penguin Group (Australia), 250 Camberwell Road, Camberwell, Victoria 3124, Australia
(a division of Pearson Australia Group Pty. Ltd.)
Penguin Books India Pvt. Ltd., 11 Community Centre, Panchsheel Park, New Delhi—110 017, India
Penguin Group (NZ), 67 Apollo Drive, Rosedale, North Shore 0632, New Zealand
(a division of Pearson New Zealand Ltd.)
Penguin Books, Rosebank Office Park, 181 Jan Smuts Avenue, Parktown North 2193, South Africa
Penguin China, B7 Jaiming Center, 27 East Third Ring Road North,
Chaoyang District, Beijing 100020, China

Penguin Books Ltd., Registered Offices: 80 Strand, London WC2R 0RL, England

Text copyright © 2010 Sue Bentley. Illustrations copyright © 2010 Angela Swan. Cover illustration
© 2010 Andrew Farley. First printed in Great Britain in 2010 by Puffin Books. First published in the
United States in 2013 by Grosset & Dunlap, a division of Penguin Young Readers Group,
345 Hudson Street, New York, New York 10014. GROSSET & DUNLAP
is a trademark of Penguin Group (USA) Inc. Printed in the U.S.A.

Library of Congress Cataloging-in-Publication Data is available.

ISBN 978-0-448-46729-0   10 9 8 7 6 5 4 3 2

ALWAYS LEARNING   PEARSON

Please help the bunnies of Moonglow Meadow!

Our brave and loyal friend, Arrow, has traveled far from our world to protect the magic key that keeps our kingdom safe from the dark rabbits. Arrow is very far from home and will need your help.

Could you be his friend?

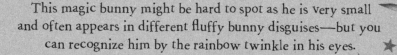

This magic bunny might be hard to spot as he is very small and often appears in different fluffy bunny disguises—but you can recognize him by the rainbow twinkle in his eyes.

Thank you for your help!

Strike
Leader of Moonglow Meadow

Prologue

Arrow glanced around Moonglow Meadow as he emerged from the burrow. A rainbow shone in his warm brown eyes as he looked at the lush grass, dotted with colorful wildflowers. All around him, other magic rabbits were eating or drinking from the crystal pool.

It was good to be back.

Arrow shook himself and his velvety white fur ruffled up before settling into place again. He stretched out happily on the warm grass. Sunlight gleamed on the tiny gold key that Arrow wore on a fine chain around his neck. As guardian of Moonglow Meadow, it was his responsibility to keep it safe.

A large older rabbit with a wise expression and a dark gray muzzle bounded up to him.

"Strike!" Arrow bowed in greeting before the leader of the warren.

"I am sorry to disturb your rest when you have only just returned," Strike said gravely. "But I wanted to warn you—the dark rabbits are coming to try to steal the magic key."

The deep gully next to Moonglow

Meadow was home to a neighboring
warren of fierce dark rabbits. Their land
had become dry and nothing could
grow there, so they were hungry.

Arrow felt a stir of dismay. "But why
can't they share our land?"

Strike shook his head sadly. "I am
afraid they refuse to do so. They want
to use our magic key to make their land
lush and green again."

Arrow gave a gasp of horror. "But
then Moonglow Meadow will become a
desert and we will starve!"

"Yes. That is why you must go to
the Otherworld. Hide there with the
key, so the dark rabbits cannot find it."

Arrow tried not to think of all the
dangers he might face. Taking a deep
breath, he lifted his head. "I will do it."

Strike's old face creased with pride. "We chose well when we made you guardian of our key. You must leave at once." He gave a soft but piercing cry.

All the rabbits pricked up their ears and rushed to form a circle around Arrow. Suddenly, the golden key glowed brightly, like a miniature sun. The light slowly faded and where the young magic rabbit had been, now stood a tiny fluffy caramel-brown-and-white bunny with brown eyes that gleamed with tiny rainbows.

"Use this disguise. Return only when Moonglow Meadow needs more of the key's magic," Strike ordered. "And watch out for dark rabbits."

Arrow raised his little fluffy chin proudly. "I will!"

Thud. Thud. Thud. The rabbits
thumped their feet in time. Arrow felt
the magic building and a cloud of crystal
dust sparkled around him as Moonglow
Meadow began to fade . . .

Chapter
ONE

"Bye, Dad! Don't forget to give Mom a big hug from me when you get back!" Charlotte Denman leaned down to kiss her dad good-bye through the open car window.

Mr. Denman smiled. "I will. Don't worry, she's going to be fine," he said gently. "Now, you and Mel must have a lot of catching-up to do. Just concentrate on having a good time. Okay?"

Charlotte nodded, smiling. Since
Mom had gotten sick a few months
ago, Charlotte hadn't been able to stop
worrying about when she would get
better. Mom had finished her treatment
now and was resting at home, but she
was still very thin and pale. "See you
both in a few days."

She stood waving until the car was no
longer in sight, then walked back toward

her friend who was standing at the gate of her front garden. The worry she was still feeling about her mom faded a bit as she saw Mel's smiling face. This was the first time she'd seen her best friend since Mel had moved nearly six months ago. She'd missed her a lot and had been looking forward to her trip for ages.

"I'm so glad you could come!" Mel's blue eyes were shining as Charlotte reached her. Her dark hair was pulled away from her pretty round face.

"Me too," Charlotte said. "Wow! Your hair's gotten really long."

"I know!" Mel flipped her ponytail over one shoulder. "Shows how long it's been since we moved here."

"Tell me about it!" Charlotte joked, rolling her eyes. "It feels like ten years."

They both laughed.

Charlotte still really missed Mel, who used to live down the street when they'd both lived in the same town. They'd been in the same class at school since they were five years old and used to spend all their spare time together. They'd even been on vacation with each other's families.

A warm breeze stirred Charlotte's short red hair as she and Mel walked toward the cottage. It had pink walls and a thatched roof and tulips, bluebells, and other spring flowers filled the pretty front yard. Seagulls wheeled overhead.

"How are Clover and Daisy?" Charlotte asked eagerly. She had a bag of treats in her suitcase for Mel's adorable gray rabbits.

"Oh, you know. They're just the same," Mel said vaguely. "Come on. I'll show you around."

Inside the cottage, the downstairs rooms all had white walls and wooden ceiling beams. Colorful rugs covered the stone floors and there was a huge fireplace in the living room. Charlotte could imagine how cozy it would be with a big log fire burning there on cold evenings. It couldn't be more different from her house back in town.

Mel led the way upstairs. "Mom's put

you in the attic room. It's a bit small but it looks out on the backyard. I hope you like it."

Charlotte's eyes widened as she opened her bedroom door. A small desk and chair stood beside a chest of drawers. A big comfy-looking brass bed took up most of one wall. Its cheerful yellow and white spotted quilt matched the curtains. "Oh, it's gorgeous. I love it!"

Her suitcase stood on the rug, where her dad had placed it earlier. Charlotte walked past it and glanced out of the window at the lawn and flowerbeds. A wooden building was visible between the trees.

"Is that where Clover and Daisy live?" she asked Mel.

Mel nodded. "That's the old barn. Dad's made it into a workshop."

"Let's go and see them." Charlotte was looking forward to making a fuss of the rabbits and playing with them, just like she and Mel used to.

Mel didn't look that happy. She shrugged. "If you really want to."

"I do!" Charlotte said firmly, giving her a friendly dig in the ribs.

They trudged downstairs and went through the kitchen into the large backyard. As they entered the barn, Charlotte wrinkled her nose at the smell of dirty straw. The rabbit cage needed cleaning.

"Hello, girls!" She poked a finger through the mesh to stroke each of the gray rabbits. They snuffled her fingers through the wire mesh, pink noses twitching curiously.

To her dismay Charlotte saw that their food dish was empty and the water bottle needed refilling. She frowned. It wasn't like Mel to be so careless.

Mel must have seen the look on her face. "I've been extra busy lately," she said quickly. "I was going to clean the cage out today, but then I was so excited about you coming that I forgot."

"Why don't we do it together?" Charlotte suggested. "It'll be fun. I miss cuddling Daisy and Clover."

Mel shifted her feet reluctantly. "What, right now? I'm expecting Jamelia and Kay to call me any minute."

"Who are they?"

"Two girls from my new school. They

live in the village. I told them you were coming and they're really looking forward to meeting you and doing stuff together."

Charlotte hid her surprise. She'd expected the two of them to spend the week together on their own, just like they used to. "No offense, but I was looking forward to it being just us," she said, feeling a bit awkward. "We never needed to be with anyone else to have fun before. Besides, we promised we'd *always* be best friends, didn't we?"

"Well, yeah. But that doesn't mean we can't have other friends, too, does it?" Mel asked hesitantly.

No, except that I haven't made any new friends, Charlotte thought sadly. Mel seemed to have moved on and made new friends without any problem. But

Charlotte hadn't felt like doing that, with her mom being so sick. Besides, she hadn't met anyone she liked nearly as much as Mel. She felt a bit hurt that Mel obviously didn't feel the same way.

Swallowing hard, Charlotte forced a smile. "No, you're right. I guess it will be fun to meet your new friends. Where do you keep the rabbit stuff?" she asked quickly, changing the subject.

Mel's face cleared and she smiled back. "It's in here." Opening a cupboard beneath the cage, she took out bags of hay and straw.

Charlotte was unlatching the cage door when Mel's mom popped her head inside the barn door.

"Hi, girls. Having fun? Jamelia's on the phone, Mel. She just called."

Mel's face lit up. "Okay. Thanks, Mom." She thrust the bags at Charlotte and raced toward her mom. "Back in a minute!" she called over her shoulder.

Left alone, Charlotte's shoulders slumped. "Looks like it's just you and me then, girls," she sighed. She gave Daisy and Clover the rabbit treats she'd bought from the pet store back home. As she stroked them, she noticed there were knots in their long gray fur and they needed a good brushing. Charlotte frowned. Mel always used to love looking after her rabbits and making a big fuss of them. What was going on?

Suddenly, there was a bright flash and a shower of crystal dust drifted down around the cage like a twinkling cloud.

"Oh!" Charlotte narrowed her eyes, trying to make sense of what she was seeing.

As the strange mist slowly cleared, she spotted a tiny fluffy caramel-brown-and-white bunny hopping out from behind Daisy.

"Can you help me, please?" the bunny asked in a scared little voice.

Chapter TWO

Charlotte stared at the cute little bunny in complete astonishment. Its face, ears, and body were a warm caramel-brown color and it had a broad white stripe down its nose. One of its front paws and its little chest were also white.

Why hadn't Mel told her that she had a new bunny? It must have been hiding at the back of the cage the whole time. Charlotte smiled at herself for imagining things. Little fluffy bunnies, however cute, couldn't talk!

"Hello. Aren't you gorgeous?" she said gently. Despite being so tiny, it didn't seem to be scared of her. "I wonder what Mel calls you."

The caramel-brown-and-white bunny twitched its little ears curiously and looked up at her with dewy brown eyes.

"I do not know anyone called Mel. My name is Arrow. I am guardian of

Moonglow Meadow," it said, squaring its fluffy little shoulders proudly.

"You really *can* talk! I wasn't imagining it!" Charlotte gasped. She felt like pinching herself to make sure she wasn't dreaming.

"Yes. All of my warren can talk," Arrow told her. "May I know your name?"

"Um . . . yeah. I'm Charlotte. Charlotte Denman. I'm here visiting my best friend."

"I am honored to meet you, Charlotte." Arrow hopped closer to the open cage door and bowed his head. As he straightened up again, a rainbow shone in his brown eyes.

"Me too." She bowed awkwardly, not sure whether she ought to curtsy

or something. She still couldn't
quite believe this was happening. "Is
Moonglow Meadow near Mel's village?"

"No. It is far away. In another
world." Arrow shook his head and
something around his neck twinkled.
Charlotte saw that he wore a tiny gold
key on a fine gold chain.

"Is that a good-luck charm?" she
asked.

"It is a magic key that keeps
Moonglow Meadow lush and green. I
must guard it from our neighbors, the
dark rabbits, who want to steal it."

Charlotte frowned. "Why would they
want to do that?"

"Their land has become dry. Nothing
grows there anymore and they are
hungry. But they refuse to share our

land. They want to use the key's magic to make their land green again, but Moonglow Meadow would become a desert if that happened."

"Oh no!" Charlotte exclaimed. "That would be awful."

Arrow's fluffy little face creased in determination. "Yes! That is why I agreed to come here and keep it safe."

Charlotte was still having trouble
believing this was really happening, but
she was fascinated by Arrow's world. It
sounded so strange and magical.

She smiled warmly at the brave
little bunny. "That sounds like a scary
mission for someone so tiny."

Arrow raised himself up onto his
back legs. His whiskers twitched
mischievously.

"Please stand back," he ordered.

The tiny bunny leaped out of the
cage and landed on the barn floor in
front of her. She felt a strange warm
tingling sensation down her spine as the
key around Arrow's neck began to glow
brightly and a cloud of twinkling crystal
dust appeared and swirled around him.
When it cleared, Charlotte saw that the

little caramel-brown-and-white bunny had disappeared. Standing in front of her was the most magnificent rabbit she had ever seen. It was the size of a large cat and had silky snowy-white fur flecked with silver. The tips of its large upright ears looked as if they'd been dipped in silver.

Charlotte gasped.

"Arrow?" she gulped.

"Yes, Charlotte. It is still me," Arrow said in a rich velvety voice. A rainbow twinkled in his chocolate-brown eyes.

Before she could get used to seeing him in his true form, there was a final glow of light from his key and Arrow reappeared as a tiny fluffy caramel-brown-and-white bunny.

"That's an amazing disguise!"

Charlotte exclaimed.

Arrow flattened his little ears nervously. "The dark rabbits will not be fooled if they discover me. I must hide, and quickly."

Charlotte's heart went out to the brave little bunny, who was so far from home. "I've got a lovely room at the top of the house. You can stay there with me. Wait until Mel hears about you—"

"No, I am sorry, Charlotte. You can tell no one about me. My mission must remain a secret," the magic bunny said seriously. "Please, promise me."

Charlotte fought her dismay. She was hoping that once Mel met this magic bunny, she might remember the fun they used to have, and that they would be able to play with Arrow together. But it was more important to keep Arrow safe from his enemies.

"Okay. No one will ever hear about you from me," she said. "As soon as I've finished cleaning Daisy and Clover's cage, I'll smuggle you up to my bedroom."

"Thank you, Charlotte. I would like that very much." Arrow leaped up into her arms in another little cloud of sparkling crystal dust.

"Oh!" Charlotte closed her hands gently around his furry little body as he snuggled close to her. She loved the idea of having an amazing secret friend of her own. Maybe with Arrow to keep her company, she wouldn't mind quite so much that Mel was spending time with her new friends instead of her.

Chapter THREE

"Sorry I took so long," Mel apologized as she came back into the barn. "The minute I hung up with Jamelia, Kay called. They can't wait to meet you. Wow! The cage looks great."

"I gave Clover and Daisy some food and refilled the water bottle, too," Charlotte said, deliberately standing in front of Arrow, who was hopping around on the floor, nibbling some hay she'd dropped. It was amazing that Mel hadn't noticed him yet. "Um . . . what should I do with this garbage bag of smelly straw?"

"It can go on Dad's compost heap." Mel looked a bit sheepish as she grasped the full bag. "Do you mind if we don't mention that you cleaned the cage? Mom and Dad have been nagging me to do it for ages. I guess I've just been busy with other things, but I'm going to try to make more of an effort—starting now!"

"Um . . . okay. Fine by . . . um . . . me," Charlotte agreed distractedly as she watched Arrow hopping toward the open door. Mel was sure to spot him any minute now.

She had to get him upstairs as quickly as she could.

"Thanks." Mel seemed relieved. "So don't you want to know what Jamelia and Kay called for? We're going to—"

"Can you tell me later?" Charlotte interrupted, edging toward the door. "I'm . . . um . . . just going to unpack my stuff."

Mel looked a bit disappointed at Charlotte's eagerness to leave. She turned around to face the cage. "Okay. Daisy and Clover need a brushing, anyway. I'll come and find you afterward," she said, picking up one of the big gray rabbits.

As soon as Mel's back was turned, Charlotte quickly scooped Arrow up, hid him in a fold of her T-shirt and hurried outside. "I don't understand why Mel didn't see you. You were right under her nose!" she said as they headed across the yard.

"I used my magic so that only you can see and hear me," Arrow explained.

"You can make yourself invisible?" Charlotte exclaimed. "Fantastic! That makes it much easier to keep you a secret!"

In the bedroom, she pulled the quilt into a cozy nest and Arrow immediately dived into it. With a contented sigh, he curled up and put his nose between his fluffy brown and white front paws.

Charlotte smiled at him as she unpacked her suitcase and stuffed her clothes into the chest of drawers. "I just had a thought. Maybe you'd prefer to live with Clover and Daisy in their nice clean cage?"

Arrow shook his head. He yawned, showing his little pink tongue. "Daisy and Clover are great rabbits. But I would much rather live with you."

"Good! I hoped you'd say that." Charlotte stroked his velvety ears. She'd only known Arrow for a short time, but she already loved him!

A little later, Charlotte heard footsteps coming up the stairs. Mel stuck her head into the room.

"Have you finished unpacking? Mom's going to treat us to lunch in the village cafe. We can stay there on our own while she does some shopping."

"Sounds great!" Charlotte jumped up eagerly. Lunch with Mel on her own was just what she needed. They could have a girlie chat, just like old times.

"Meet you outside in a minute!"

Charlotte stroked her little bunny friend. "You can stay here for a nap if you want while I go out with Mel."

Arrow jumped up and gave himself a little shake. "I am not sleepy anymore. I will come with you!"

Charlotte smiled. "I'll take my

shoulder bag. It's probably best if you get in there so you'll be safe."

She opened it and Arrow jumped inside. They went downstairs to meet Mel's mom, who was already waiting outside the house. There was no sign of a car.

"Are we walking?" Charlotte asked, surprised. Where she lived, everyone used cars, even for short journeys.

"Yes. That's what legs are for," Mrs. George joked. She had an old-fashioned wicker basket looped over one arm. "Everything's so close here in the village. We love it. By the way, how's your mom? I've been meaning to call her to see how she's doing. It's been ages since we had a good talk."

"Oh, Mom's fine," Charlotte said, forcing down a stab of worry. *At least, I hope she soon will be.* Mel's family didn't know that her mom had been sick since they left, and Charlotte didn't find it easy to talk about.

Mel joined them and they all set off. It was only two minutes to the end of the road, then they turned down another road that came out onto the main street. She glimpsed the sea and beach in the distance, between rows of charming beach huts, painted in ice-cream colors.

"The stores are here," Mel said.

They walked along a street, lined on both sides with stone houses and pink-walled cottages. Arrow was leaning up out of Charlotte's shoulder bag, his

nose twitching at all the exciting smells.
His ears swiveled at the seagulls' cries.

Charlotte was glad her bunny friend
was enjoying himself. But she couldn't
help feeling a bit disappointed. When
Mel had talked about moving to
the seashore, she had imagined cute
stores selling postcards, ice cream, and
candy. But all she could see was an
old-fashioned-looking butcher shop,

a drugstore, and another store with boxes of fruit, vegetables, and flowers in buckets on the sidewalk outside.

"What sort of place is this? I wonder what Mel does when she's not at school. There's not even a shopping center like at home," she whispered to Arrow.

But she must have spoken more loudly than she meant to. "Well, I love it here. It's much better than living in a boring old town," Mel said, going a bit red.

"The village seemed rather quiet to us, too, when we first moved here," Mel's mom said, smiling at Charlotte. "But Mel soon discovered there was a lot to do."

Charlotte bit her lip and fell silent.

She hadn't meant to upset anyone.

"Here we are!" Mel's mom exclaimed a few moments later. The cafe window was full of delicious-looking cakes. A green-and-white sign read THE PANTRY.

They found empty seats at a large table. Charlotte felt Arrow jump into her lap.

"Okay, girls. What would you like?" Mrs. George asked, handing them each a menu.

Charlotte was still trying to make up her mind about all the delicious food when Mel gave a loud shriek and leaped to her feet. "Here are Kay and Jamelia!"

Arrow almost jumped out of his fur and Charlotte had to hold him tight so he didn't escape in a panic. His little heart ticked against her hand. "It's okay. Nothing to be scared of," she whispered. When she looked up again, two girls had come into the cafe.

"Charlotte, this is Jamelia and Kay!" Mel introduced her friends. "I know I didn't tell you we were meeting them, but I wanted it to be a surprise."

"Oh, okay. Um . . . hi!" Charlotte said, her heart sinking as she tried not to feel too disappointed that she wouldn't be spending the time alone with Mel. Beneath the table, she was still stroking Arrow gently until he gradually calmed down.

"It's nice to meet you," Jamelia said. She had olive skin and shiny black hair, which she wore in a long braid.

"Me too—Mel's told us so much

about you!" Kay had a wide smile and a friendly heart-shaped face. She peered at Charlotte through wispy blond bangs.

"So, what's everyone having?" Mel's mom stood up. Once they'd decided what they wanted, she went to the counter to order their food.

"How was drama class this morning?" Mel asked her new friends.

"It was hilarious!" Jamelia rolled her eyes dramatically. "We had to pretend

to be trees. We waved our arms like branches and tried to talk to each other without making sounds. You should have seen Emma. She's got really long arms, anyway . . ."

Jamelia demonstrated by making a face and then spreading her fingers and holding up bent arms. Mel and Kay started laughing. Charlotte smiled politely, although she couldn't see the point of acting like a tree! She didn't remember Mel liking drama when they'd been at school together. They'd always preferred playing in the tree house in Mel's large backyard, sometimes even camping out there when it was warm.

"I wish I'd been there!" Mel said. "But I had to stay at home to meet Charlotte."

"Sorry I made you miss it," Charlotte murmured.

But no one seemed to hear her. Mel, Jamelia, and Kay giggled as they talked about all the things they usually did together at drama class and sports practice. Mel had apparently started taking horseback-riding lessons, too.

Charlotte smiled and tried to seem interested, but felt a little left out of the conversation. Mel seemed to have such an exciting new life, completely different from the one she had back home. No wonder she didn't miss the things she and Charlotte used to do together.

Charlotte stroked her magic bunny's little soft ears, glad she had Arrow to keep her company. She cheered up a bit when her chocolate milkshake and

hamburger arrived. They were delicious.
She'd asked for extra lettuce and tomato
on the side and no one noticed when
she slipped pieces into her lap. Arrow
soon polished off the tomato and two
enormous lettuce leaves. Charlotte bit
back a grin as she felt his soft little
mouth nudging her fingers.

"So are you looking forward
to playing tennis later?" Mel asked
Charlotte. "The grass courts in the park
are great. We play all the time. I tried
to mention it to you earlier, just before
you went upstairs to unpack."

"Tennis?" Surely Mel remembered
how much she hated sports? She'd never
realized Mel liked tennis, either. "But
I didn't bring any gym stuff with me,"
Charlotte said hastily. "I'll just watch."

"No problem. I have a spare racket you can use," Kay said.

"Oh, okay. Thanks," Charlotte said without enthusiasm. *Great. Now I can't even get out of it.*

Mel's mom went off to do her shopping, leaving Charlotte and Arrow in the cafe with Mel, Kay, and Jamelia.

"Let's get more milkshakes. My treat," Jamelia said, jumping up. "You have to try the strawberry, Charlotte. It's so yummy!"

"Okay. Thanks," Charlotte said, smiling.

Mel's new friends were really nice and she liked them both. But she still wished that she could have her old best friend to herself, at least on her first day here. She couldn't help feeling a little bit envious that Mel had found such great friends, especially since she herself had been too worried about her mom to think about forming other friendships at home.

Her magic bunny was a warm, comforting weight in her lap. Charlotte stroked Arrow's velvety caramel ears, glad that he was her own special friend and she would never have to share him with anybody.

Chapter
FOUR

"Phew! Now I remember why I
hate tennis so much!" Charlotte said to
Arrow that evening.

They had left Kay and Jamelia at the
park and walked back to the cottage
after their game. Charlotte was hot and
sweaty and had gone straight up to her
bedroom to change.

Arrow was stretched out on the

quilt, with his front paws crossed. He watched as Charlotte picked irritably at a strand of damp red hair that was sticking to her hot face.

"Look at me. I look like a tomato! And I was *so* terrible," she groaned. "I've got the worst serve in the universe, especially compared to Kay and Jamelia."

"They are very nice girls. I like them," Arrow said.

"Me too. Bad luck," Charlotte grumbled. She had to admit that Jamelia and Kay had been encouraging and patient, despite the fact that she'd barely managed to get the ball over the net. "But I couldn't keep up a single volley for more than ten seconds. I bet they're laughing about how horrible I was."

The magic bunny twitched his whiskers sympathetically. "No one can be good at everything."

"I guess not." Charlotte smiled at her loyal little friend as she pulled off her sweaty T-shirt. After a quick splash of water, she put on a clean top and sat on the bed. "I guess I'm just a bit sad that Mel's doing all this new stuff without me. I never knew that she wanted to go to drama classes and horseback ride. She must think I'm really boring now."

"Perhaps you could talk to her," Arrow suggested.

Charlotte shook her head sadly. "I don't want her to feel bad. She has been nice about sharing her new friends with me. I guess I should try to get used to things being different between

Mel and me now. But it's really hard since we used to be so close," she sighed.

"I will help you in any way I can. I am your friend!" Arrow raised himself up on his back legs and rested his fluffy front paws on her bare arm.

"Same goes for me," she said fondly. Turning toward him, she touched his little white paw with a fingertip. "Will we be friends forever?"

"Yes!" Arrow's big brown eyes gleamed with tiny rainbows. "Even when I have to leave."

"Leave?" Charlotte echoed. "I . . . I was hoping you'd come back home and live with me. We have a nice house with a big backyard. There are tons of dandelion leaves and other things for you to eat."

"I am afraid that is not possible, Charlotte," Arrow said gently. "When the magic key glows, it will mean that Moonglow Meadow is in need of more magic. I may have to leave suddenly, without saying good-bye."

Charlotte swallowed her sadness and forced herself to look on the bright side. "Maybe the last bit of magic will keep working for a long time." She couldn't bear to think of losing Arrow. His friendship meant so much to her, especially whenever she thought about Mel and her new friends.

"Perhaps. I will stay with you for as long as I can," Arrow promised.

Reassured, Charlotte decided not to think about it anymore and to try to enjoy every single moment with her magical friend.

Charlotte came downstairs the following morning with Arrow tucked invisibly beneath one arm. Mel was sitting at the breakfast table. Her dad was there as well, reading the paper. A delicious smell of eggs and breakfast sausage filled the kitchen.

"Hi!" Mel looked up and smiled as Charlotte sat down and settled the magic bunny on her lap.

Mr. George looked at her over the top of his paper. "So, did you girls have a nice time yesterday?" he asked.

Mel answered before Charlotte could reply. "It was great!" She told him about the cafe lunch and meeting Jamelia and Kay. "It was Jamelia's idea to play tennis in the afternoon. I told her I was worried that Charlotte would get bored hanging around the village."

"It is very quiet," Mel's dad agreed. "It took Mel a while to get used to it and find new friends, didn't it?"

Mel nodded. "But there're lots of things to do here, once you know where to go. Maybe we could go to the carnival at the beach tomorrow?"

Charlotte smiled, feeling happier knowing Mel still wanted to spend time

with her. It sounded like the three girls
had teamed up just to make sure she
had a good time.

She turned to Mel. "Thanks for
yesterday. I did have fun. Sorry if I was
a bit grumpy before. And thanks again
for treating us to lunch, Mrs. George."

"You're welcome," Mel's mom said
from across the kitchen. "You did seem
to have something on your mind. Is
everything all right, honey?"

"Yeah, fine," Charlotte said, feeling
much better. The nagging worry about

her mom was still there, though. She decided she would call her later.

Mel's mom put a plate of hot buttery toast on the table. "Breakfast sausages, toast, and eggs okay for everyone?"

"Yes, please," Mel and Charlotte chorused.

"I thought we could go to the beach later," Mel said to Charlotte, munching her toast. "Kay and Jamelia are coming over in an hour."

"Good idea," her dad agreed. "It's not warm enough to sit around. But you can all go on a nice walk."

Charlotte couldn't help a slight sinking feeling at having to share Mel again with her new friends. But it might be more fun this time if she made an effort to join in.

The phone rang in the hall and Mel's mom hurried to answer it.

"That'll be Grandma," Mel said. "She always calls on Saturday mornings."

Mel's dad started telling them a funny story about something that happened at work. He was a nurse and had transferred to the emergency room at the local hospital. Charlotte had always loved hearing about the medical dramas. She and Mel were listening so closely that no one noticed the burning smell coming from the stove until the smoke detector made a loud beeping noise.

"Oh no! The sausages!" Mel's dad jumped to his feet and dashed over to the stove. He grabbed the smoking pan

and rushed outside into the backyard.
A few moments later, he came back
in empty-handed. "Sorry, girls," he
groaned. "I'm afraid they're too burned
to eat."

"Oh my goodness. What on earth's
going on?" Mel's mom came back into
the kitchen.

"The sausages caught on fire," Mel
said, giggling uncontrollably. "Dad threw
them into the yard!"

"Mel's being dramatic. I didn't throw them anywhere!" her dad said, starting to laugh. "I took the pan outside to help get rid of the smoke." He started fanning a dishcloth beneath the smoke alarm.

Charlotte was spluttering with laughter, too. "What a shame! I was really looking forward to those sausages," she whispered to Arrow when she could finally speak.

Arrow twitched his whiskers mischievously. He jumped onto the floor and raised himself up onto his back legs. Charlotte noticed the gold key around his neck flashing.

She felt a warm tingling sensation down her spine and a cloud of sparkling crystal dust appeared and floated out of the open kitchen door. It was just visible through the window, whirling in the air above something, before apparently floating down and disappearing with a loud sizzling sound.

"Arrow? What did you just do?" Charlotte whispered suspiciously.

The magic bunny held his fluffy front paws up to his face and looked over them innocently. Charlotte's lips twitched as she only just managed not to burst out laughing again. Arrow looked so naughty and cute.

Mel's mom had gone into the yard. She came back in carrying the pan. "I don't know what all the fuss was about. These sausages are perfectly cooked."

Mel's dad scratched his head in puzzlement. "So they are. I could have sworn they were burned to a crisp! I must have been imagining things. That smoke alarm needs checking."

His wife gave him a look. "Maybe it's your eyesight that needs checking!"

Everyone burst out laughing.

Charlotte smiled at her fluffy, wide-eyed little friend. "That was really sneaky, Arrow!"

Chapter
FIVE

Charlotte ran upstairs to change her shoes and grab her bag and jacket before Kay and Jamelia arrived to go to the beach.

There was just enough time to call her mom, so she asked if she could use the phone. It rang for a long time and Charlotte was about to hang up when her mom answered.

"Hi, Mom! It's me!"

"Hello, honey. Sorry I took a while to answer. I was just listening to one of my relaxation CDs."

"Are you feeling better?" Charlotte asked quietly. She didn't want Mel or her mom and dad to hear and start asking awkward questions.

"Getting there slowly, but I won't be running a marathon for a while!" she joked. "How are you and Mel doing?"

"Fine. I love the cottage and my room's beautiful!" Charlotte told her about their plans to go to the beach. "We're going with Kay and Jamelia. They're Mel's new friends."

"Sounds good. Are they nice girls?"

"Yes, they are. I like them both," she said after a pause.

"But you hadn't expected Mel to have made such good friends so soon?" her mom guessed.

Charlotte blinked in surprise. "How did you know that?"

"I know you, Charlotte Denman. You always had to have the same story over and over again when you were little. And you've still got all your old dolls and teddy bears. You like things to stay the way they are."

"I guess I do," Charlotte admitted.

"That's fine," her mom said, "and I know you've really missed Mel since she left. But you can't expect her not to meet other people—she has a new life now. It's actually nice of her to want to share them with you."

"I guess," Charlotte murmured.

She was beginning to think that her mom was right. Maybe when she got back home she would feel more like forming new friendships of her own, like Mel had. But it was great to have Arrow with her until then. He was a very special friend.

She heard her mom take a deep breath. She didn't want to tire her out with talking. "You should rest, Mom. I'll call you again tomorrow."

"Hey, who's the mom here?" her mom laughed. "You have a good time on the beach."

"I will. Take care. Love you, Mom."

"Love you, too."

She sighed as she picked up her bag. Arrow was sitting up, looking out of it.

"Is something wrong, Charlotte?"

"It's Mom—" Charlotte hesitated, but she felt like she could tell Arrow anything. She took a deep breath. "Mom's been really sick. She's had weeks of treatment. The doctors say she'll get better now, but I'm . . . I'm scared that she won't."

"Does Mel know this?" Arrow asked.

Charlotte shook her head. "No one except my family knows. I don't want to talk about it in case I get upset. But it's different with you somehow."

"I am glad that you told me," Arrow said gently, rubbing his soft caramel-colored cheek against her hand.

Charlotte stroked him. "Me too. Now you're keeping my secret, just like I'm keeping yours."

He looked at her face again. "Yes. But perhaps it might help if you talked to Mel about this."

Charlotte shook her head. "I don't want her feeling sorry for me. Or being extra nice to me just because Mom's sick. I'd rather not say anything."

Just then the doorbell rang and Mel came running from the kitchen

past Charlotte and Arrow to open it.
"Kay and Jamelia are here! Ready,
Charlotte?"

"Coming." Slipping her bag over
her shoulder, Charlotte followed Mel
outside and said hello to Kay and
Jamelia. They all walked toward the
beach. Weak sunshine shone through
the clouds and a stiff breeze whipped
Charlotte's hair across her face. Arrow
ducked down inside her bag to stay
warm.

Charlotte was looking forward to her
first visit to the beach. So far, she'd only
had a brief glimpse of it. She imagined
soft sand, a pretty curving bay, and
maybe even rock pools to investigate.
But as they reached the beach, she
gave a cry of surprise. "Oh no! It's all

pebbles!"

Mel frowned. "Yeah. So what?"

"Well, pebbles aren't as good as
sand. They hurt your bare feet and you
can't build sandcastles or anything."
Charlotte glanced at Mel, who looked
offended. She suddenly wished she'd
kept her mouth shut, but it was too
late now.

"My dad says it's good for your feet,
like having a massage," Jamelia said
cheerfully. "We do lots of stuff on the
beach like skipping stones and treasure
hunts. I have my kite with me. You
can fly it, if you want."

"Thanks. I'd like that." Charlotte
grinned, remembering her promise to
make the best of things.

But Mel still looked annoyed.

Stuffing her hands in her jeans pockets, she strode ahead.

Charlotte trudged along, the pebbles crunching beneath her sneakers. A few feet away, the beach sloped sharply toward the gray sea, where sluggish waves collapsed on the shore. A row of boats was moored at the far end. She could see their rusting anchors sticking out of the pebbles and the big loops of blue rope, draped with strands of seaweed.

Mel's hair whipped around her face as the group made their way along the pebbles. "It so windy today. I wish I'd brought my kite, too!"

Kay ran ahead of them, spreading her arms. "Let's pretend to be kites being blown around by the wind!"

While the three of them laughed and ran along the water, Charlotte hung back feeling nervous about joining in with their game. Perhaps all being friends together wasn't going to be as easy as she thought. Mel and her new friends seemed to enjoy doing such different things to her. She turned to Arrow. "I don't think you'll be able to hop around on these pebbles. Maybe you'd better stay in my bag."

"I will be fine!" Arrow pricked his ears excitedly.

Charlotte felt a faint warm prickling sensation again and saw his key flashing as he jumped down in a swirl of crystal dust. He landed on a sort of invisible sparkly magic carpet. It unfurled in

front of him as he moved forward
and snuffled about. Charlotte smiled at
her magic bunny. His little paws were
cushioned from the cold hard stones.

Jamelia ran back to Charlotte and
took a fold-up kite out of her pocket.
She assembled it and then handed
Charlotte the plastic handle, which was
attached to a spool of thread. "Come
on! Let's fly a *real* kite!" she said.

"What do I have to do?" Charlotte
asked.

Jamelia showed her how to run along
the beach, holding up the kite so it
trailed behind her. She gave the kite to
Charlotte, who ran back to where Arrow
was busy investigating some of the larger
pebbles on the beach. Mel, Jamelia, and
Kay were left far behind her.

Charlotte laughed with delight as the kite lifted a few inches into the air.

"I think I'm getting the hang of this," she cried excitedly.

Arrow had stopped to watch her. His eyes fastened on the orange-and-purple kite and the long crinkly tail fluttering out behind it. His little bobtail swiveled in fascination. Suddenly, a particularly strong gust of wind took hold of the kite. It was jerked out of Charlotte's hand and went twisting and tumbling down the beach.

Arrow dashed headlong after it, his little floppy ears swept backward.

Charlotte's heart missed a beat. Arrow thought it was a game. He'd probably never seen a kite and would follow it right up until it plunged into the water!

"Arrow! Stop," she warned. "It's too dangerous!"

But it was too late. A huge wave was rolling toward the shore. It looked just about to break. The way Arrow was tearing along, he'd be directly in its path!

Chapter SIX

"Oh no!" Charlotte thought quickly. She had to get to him. Leaping forward, she ran as fast as she could toward the shore. The rushing sound of the waves came closer.

Arrow was running around, trying to nip at the kite's trailing tail. He had no idea of the danger he was in. Charlotte's heart was in her mouth.

"Arrow! Come back!" she yelled.

But the wind seemed to snatch her
voice and he didn't hear her.

She put on another burst of speed,
slipping and sliding down the slope.
The kite swooped upward and then a
strong gust of wind blew it out to sea.
A huge wave crashed onto the shore
and the waves rushed toward Arrow. At
the last moment, he seemed to realize
his danger and froze in terror.

Charlotte gave a desperate lurch
forward. She stretched out one arm
and just managed to grab Arrow by the
scruff of his neck. "Got you!"

She twisted, cushioning Arrow
against her chest as freezing cold
seawater swirled around her, soaking
her almost up to the waist. She had

somehow managed to keep Arrow dry,
but she was gasping with cold as she
turned and waded through the sea and
back to dry land.

"Are you okay?" she asked
worriedly. She couldn't stop shivering
and her teeth were chattering.

Arrow's little ears were flattened in
terror and he was trembling with shock,
but he nodded. "Thank you for saving
me. You were very brave."

"Not really. I just couldn't bear for anything to happen to you," she said, still shivering as she cradled him in her arms.

Arrow lifted his head. "You are cold. I will help you."

Charlotte felt a familiar tingling sensation down her back as Arrow's key flashed. A small cloud of crystal dust appeared and swirled around her for a few seconds, gleaming with tiny rainbows. Her clothes warmed up right away and she felt as if she was sitting in a nice hot bath. She gave a final shiver and realized that her jeans and sneakers were all dry and clean as if they had come out of the dryer at home.

"Wow! I'm completely dry now! Thanks, Arrow."

As she stood up slowly with Arrow tucked safely beneath one arm, Kay, Mel, and Jamelia came running across the pebbles toward her.

Kay reached her first. "What happened?"

"Um . . . I . . . was . . ." Charlotte floundered, unable to explain that her invisible magic bunny had been in terrible danger. "I dropped the handle of the kite and it blew away. I thought I could catch it before it reached the water—but I was running so fast that I couldn't stop myself!"

"You should be soaked," Kay said, looking puzzled. "We saw you get caught by those waves."

"The sun must be hotter than it looks," Charlotte said, thinking quickly.

"I'm hardly wet at all."

"Oh no, look at my kite!" Jamelia cried.

Everyone seemed to forget about Charlotte's amazing quick-drying clothes as they all looked out to sea, where a tangled orange-and-purple object was sinking into the dark water. It bobbed sadly on the gray waves as it was carried out by the tide.

"I'm really sorry," Charlotte said quietly. "The wind was just too strong. I'll buy you a new kite. I promise."

"That's okay. It didn't cost that much," Jamelia said.

"Don't look so upset, Charlotte. Anyone can have an accident," Kay said.

"Stop being so nice to her, you two!" Mel burst out. "Can't you see that she just wants us to fuss over her?"

"I do not!" Charlotte exclaimed, stung.

Mel put her hands on her hips. Her face was flushed with annoyance. "Yes, you do. You've had a long face since you got here. You can't say anything nice about the village, and I know you don't like it that I've made new friends here. Why can't you just be happy for me?"

Charlotte was surprised. They'd never argued like this before. There was an uncomfortable feeling in her stomach as Mel's accusations hit home. She had to admit that she'd been a bit quiet at first, but things were different now.

"Mel doesn't mean it. She'll calm down in a minute," Kay said.

Jamelia looked at Mel and then back
at Charlotte. "Kay's right. Come on,
you two. This is silly. Be friends?"

Charlotte swallowed hard. She
wanted to make up with Mel, but she
couldn't seem to find the right words.
Worse still, she felt her eyes pricking
with tears as her secret worries about
her mom suddenly surfaced. How had

everything turned into such a mess?

"I'm not feeling very well. I think I'll go back to the cottage. I . . . I'll see you later," she called, already jogging away in the direction of the village.

By the time Charlotte turned onto the road and saw the pink walls and thatched roof of Mel's cottage, she was calmer and felt a bit silly for running off. "I should have apologized to Mel and made up. Now she hates me, and Jamelia and Kay will think I'm horrible!"

"I do not believe any of them will think that," Arrow said.

Charlotte hung her head. "It would be my own fault if they did. I haven't been much fun, but I didn't think Mel would notice because she was too

busy spending time with Jamelia and
Kay. Maybe I'll tell her about Mom
being sick when she gets back from the
beach."

Arrow looked up at her with
chocolate-brown eyes. "That is a good
idea. It is never too late for a fresh
start."

Charlotte gathered her wise little
bunny in her arms and gave him a hug.
He was the best kind of friend—the
sort who made you feel better about
yourself.

Having made the decision to speak to
Mel about her mom, Charlotte's heart
felt lighter as she approached the cottage.
Then she had a sudden thought. "Mel's
mom's going to wonder why I came
back by myself. Let's go to the barn

until Mel gets back. I bet you'd like to see Clover and Daisy again, wouldn't you?"

Arrow nodded.

Opening the gate, Charlotte slipped into the backyard. In the barn, the gray rabbits came forward to look out of the wire mesh. "Hello, girls. I've brought someone to see you." Charlotte opened the cage, so Arrow could jump inside.

Lifting his fluffy head, the tiny bunny touched noses first with Daisy and then Clover. Mel's rabbits snuffled him and then both started licking him. Arrow stretched out with a blissful expression as they groomed every last bit of him.

Charlotte grinned.

She noticed that the cage was spotless and the food dish and water bottle were both full. Mel was keeping her promise about looking after the rabbits.

After a while, Arrow stood up and gave himself a little shake. Charlotte caught sight of a bag of carrots on top of the cupboard next to the cage. She took a couple out, intending to give them all a treat.

Suddenly, she heard a noise behind her. Mel's mom came into the barn, her eyebrows raised in surprise. "Hello, Charlotte. What are you doing here?"

"Waiting for Mel . . . ," she began.

"Don't tell me that you came back early to feed Mel's rabbits for her! She's got to learn to look after them herself," Mel's mom interrupted crossly.

"No, she didn't—" Charlotte began hastily, but before she could finish her sentence, a voice rang out behind her.

"I can't believe it!" Mel cried. "Now you're trying to get me into trouble with my mom and dad, too!"

Chapter SEVEN

Charlotte turned toward Mel. "I wasn't . . . I wouldn't . . ."

"Well, it doesn't look like it!" Mel said.

"That's enough, Melanie!" her mom snapped. "You can't blame Charlotte because you forgot to feed your rabbits again."

"But she di—" Charlotte tried to get
a word in edgeways.

Mel's mom held up a hand. "Don't
try to stick up for her, Charlotte. She's
been warned that we'll find a new home
for Clover and Daisy if she doesn't
take better care of them. And you're
our guest." She turned to her daughter.
"Melanie, apologize to Charlotte."

Mel glared at Charlotte. "Why should I?"

Her mom frowned. "That's enough! Go to your room!" she ordered.

Mel looked close to tears. She clenched her fists and then whirled around and ran out of the barn.

Charlotte watched her go in dismay. She felt terrible. She didn't know what to say.

"I'm sorry about that, honey," Mel's mom said. "I'd give her time to calm down, if I were you."

Charlotte nodded silently. She knew there was no point in trying to explain again. Mel's mom wouldn't believe her, anyway. She took Arrow out of the cage, while pretending to check that the door was fastened.

"Is it okay if I sit in the yard for a bit?" Charlotte asked.

Mrs. George smiled. "Of course it is. And don't worry. This will all have blown over by the morning. Weren't you supposed to be going to the carnival tomorrow?"

Charlotte nodded glumly. She couldn't imagine that Mel would want to speak to her after what had just happened. Maybe she could try once more to explain later.

But later on Mel said she wasn't feeling well, so her mom took a sandwich up to her bedroom for dinner. "I'm not going to get a chance to speak to her tonight after all," Charlotte said sadly to Arrow. "I hope she'll feel better in the morning."

Arrow nodded. "I hope so, too."

The following morning, Charlotte and Arrow made their way to the fairground, with Kay, Jamelia, Mel, and her dad all walking alongside them.

"I'm really looking forward to this. I love carnivals!" Charlotte said, smiling at Mel, who was next to her.

"Mmm." Mel nodded, but she didn't smile back.

"At least she isn't ignoring me like she was last night," Charlotte whispered to Arrow. "Perhaps we can patch things up between us during the day."

"Let's go on that first!" Kay said excitedly when they entered the park. She, Mel, and Jamelia headed straight for the biggest ride they could find. Charlotte

stood watching from the ground as the rollercoaster crept slowly up the steep, almost vertical track. Their car crested the top and paused for a moment, before whooshing downward to a deafening chorus of screams.

"Whee-ee-eee!" Mel, Jamelia, and Kay were all yelling at the top of their voices.

Charlotte waved as the girls shot past on their way to another series of dizzying swoops and dips. Arrow, who was tucked safely inside Charlotte's bag, flattened his ears in alarm as the fairground echoed with shrieks.

"It's okay. They're just having fun being scared," Charlotte whispered to him.

"Humans are very strange," he said, shaking his furry little head.

"Don't you want to give it a try?" Mel's dad asked her.

"No, thanks. I hate heights," she replied. There was no way she was taking Arrow up there. "I'll go on something else in a minute."

Colored lights flashed from the sideshows, and carnival music blared out from all the rides. The smell of frying onions, hot dogs, and cotton candy filled the air.

The roller coaster cars pulled up at the finish and there was a hissing sound as the safety bars lifted from the passengers.

Mel, Kay, and Jamelia got off, still giggling as they staggered toward Charlotte and Arrow.

"That was awesome!" Kay breathed. "What's next? The big wheel?"

"How about the ghost train?" Mel suggested. "It could be really funny!"

Charlotte smiled. The ghost train had always been her favorite ride when she'd gone to carnivals with Mel. Maybe Mel was trying to say that she'd forgiven her for what happened yesterday? "Yeah, okay," she agreed. "It'll be fun."

The ghost-train ride was painted black, with scary faces and grinning skulls. Moans and faint screams floated out of the entrance as they lined up to get in.

"This is just make-believe, with silly pretend witches and ghosts and stuff, so don't be scared," she whispered to Arrow as she sat on the train beside Mel.

"It will be interesting," Arrow said, pricking up his ears.

With a rattling noise the train moved forward and they were plunged into darkness. As they trundled along there were flashes of green light, and ghostly things jumped out of cobwebby corners or dangled from the ceiling.

Jamelia pointed at a couple of rubber bats flapping in an alcove. She spluttered with laughter.

"This is so funny!" Kay giggled as a creaky door opened to reveal a glowing plastic skeleton.

Mel pretended to yawn. "You'd have
to be about four years old to be scared. I
think I might fall asleep in a minute!"

Charlotte laughed. "It's fun, though!"
She had her bag on her lap and one hand
was inside it, resting on Arrow's little
furry back.

The train took a sudden right turn.
Nothing happened for a few seconds and
then a huge plaster rabbit with ridiculous
vampire teeth loomed toward them. A
bright light shone from behind it, casting

a long dark shadow across their car.

Arrow squealed with terror and reared up out of the bag. "My enemies have found me!"

Before Charlotte knew what was happening, his key flashed and the ghost train shuddered to a halt. There was a crackle as the power died and all the lights went out. The kids on the train started screaming. Charlotte was just about to tell Arrow there was nothing to be scared of, when she felt him jump right out of her bag and disappear into the total darkness!

Chapter
EIGHT

Charlotte peered into the darkness,
her heart beating fast. Arrow was
somewhere in the tunnel, terrified and
all alone. She had to find him, but she
knew it might be dangerous for her to
get out of the ghost train. What could
she do?

She stood up and leaned forward,
trying to catch a glimpse of her magic

bunny. Shouts and screams still rang out around her. The noise was deafening.

At least no one was going to hear if she shouted to Arrow, but hopefully he might be able to pick out her voice. It was a risk worth taking.

"Arrow! Where are you?" Charlotte yelled as loud as she could. "There are no dark rabbits here. It was just a silly game. Please come back!"

She waited, every nerve tingling with fear for her friend. Her eyes strained into the dark. There were so many places for a terrified bunny to crawl into. And the ghost train could start up again at any minute, taking her outside and leaving him in there.

"Arrow! Can you hear me?" she

shouted, cupping her
hands around her mouth.

Charlotte felt
desperate. Then all of
a sudden, she spotted
a tiny flashing light to one side of the
train. Breathing a sigh of relief, she saw
Arrow hiding behind one of the ghostly
figures.

The tunnel was illuminated as
emergency lights were switched on. A
voice came out of a loudspeaker, telling
everyone not to panic and to stay in
their seats. The kids stopped screaming
and there was a half-hearted cheer
as a side door opened and two men
appeared.

They began helping the kids off the
front of the train and steering them

toward the exit. When no one was watching, Charlotte quickly stood up and reached behind the model ghost. Her fingers brushed against Arrow's soft fur as she picked him up gently and slipped him back inside her bag.

Kay and Jamelia got up and headed for the exit, so Charlotte and Mel were the last ones on the train. They followed the other girls and all emerged together, blinking into the daylight.

"That was pretty exciting!" Mel said.

Kay laughed. "Yeah! It was much better than usual."

"Weird, wasn't it?" Charlotte said, with a glint in her eye. "Maybe there was a bit of magic about that rickety old ghost train after all."

They all laughed.

They wandered over to try their
luck at the rifle range. Charlotte hugged
Arrow while she waited her turn. "I'm
sorry you were scared," she whispered.
"I never dreamed there'd be a huge
scary rabbit in there."

He put a tiny fluffy paw on her
hand. "It is not your fault. I should not
have panicked."

Charlotte smiled at him, pleased
that he was safe. "Let's see if I can win
anything!" she said, as Mel stood back
so she could take her turn.

An hour later, Charlotte and Arrow
and the girls left the fair with Mel's dad.
Mel was clutching a giant pink bear
and Jamelia held a kite. Charlotte had

won it, but she'd given it to Jamelia to replace the one she'd lost on the beach. Charlotte stroked Arrow in her bag as they walked home.

"You look happier, Charlotte," Arrow said.

"I am!" she told him. "It was a fun day. Mel seems to have forgiven me a bit, too, even if things aren't quite back to normal yet." She had also enjoyed being with Jamelia and Kay. There was no question about it—she really did like Mel's new friends.

Charlotte woke up the next morning, looking forward to having a talk with Mel. Although the air seemed to have cleared a bit since the carnival the day before, Charlotte still wanted to talk to Mel about the situation at home, and to explain that she hadn't meant to get her into trouble with her mom.

She gathered up Arrow and headed downstairs, but when she knocked on Mel's door there was no answer. She peered into the room and saw Mel's neatly made bed, but no sign of her friend. Climbing back up the stairs toward her attic room, she wondered where Mel might be. Probably out having fun with Kay and Jamelia, she thought dejectedly.

As she went to open the door, she

caught sight of something hanging on the doorknob that she hadn't noticed earlier. It was a piece of rope, strung with six large pebbles, each with a hole through its middle. One end of the rope was formed into a loop. Charlotte picked it up by the loop and then sat down on the bed. "This wasn't here last night. I wonder what's it's for?"

"I do not know." Arrow twitched his nose. Leaping onto the bed in a shower of crystal dust, he dabbed the object with a fluffy front paw. The pebbles made a clacking sound as they rolled together.

"I thought I heard you get up." Mel walked into the room.

"They're witch stones. It's a tradition to hang them in your yard. They bring good luck."

"Witch stones?"

"That's what you call pebbles with holes through them," Mel explained. "You find them on the beach sometimes. Mom said you might like to take them home to bring you good luck."

"O-okay." Charlotte was still puzzled, but at least Mel was talking to her again. "Thanks. But how did you know I need good lu—" She paused as she realized what Mel meant. The color rushed into her cheeks. "You know about my mom?"

Mel nodded. "Mom called her when we were at the carnival yesterday and your mom told her everything. Mom explained it to me last night after you went upstairs. I got up early to go and collect these stones for you. Why didn't you say anything about her being so sick?"

Charlotte looked down at the floor. "I . . . I'm not sure. I didn't want to talk to anyone about it."

"But I'm not just anyone, am I? I thought you could trust me," Mel said, looking a bit hurt. "We used to tell each other everything."

Charlotte nodded slowly, still gazing at her sneakers. She hadn't thought of it like that. "I probably should have told you, but I got used to not wanting to talk about it. And . . . and I wanted you to know that I never said that you hadn't fed your rabbits yesterday. Your mom jumped to conclusions."

Mel smiled. "I know. We had a good talk last night. She said she might have been a bit hasty in the barn, when she thought you were feeding my rabbits for me. She believes that I'm looking after them properly again now. And I should have believed you. I know you've never been a sneak."

Charlotte let out a big sigh of relief. "So we're friends again?"

"You bet. We always will be, right?"

Charlotte nodded happily.

"How about just you and me spending the day together tomorrow?" Mel suggested.

"Sounds great!" Charlotte beamed at her, so pleased that everything was fine between them again.

Chapter
NINE

" . . . and you hang them outside
in the yard for good luck," Charlotte
finished telling her mom about the string
of lucky witch stones the next morning.

"Hmm? Unusual gift. But I think the
good luck might be working already,"
her mom said. Charlotte could tell she
was smiling.

"What do you mean?"

"Well, I'm feeling much better. I even went for a walk around the block yesterday."

"Really? That's fantastic!" Charlotte said, feeling a small glow of happiness somewhere deep inside.

"Isn't it? And I'm going out for a drive with your dad in a minute," her mom said. "Oh, I forgot to ask you, how are Clover and Daisy? I know how much you love them. Are you getting lots of bunny hugs?"

"Tons!" Charlotte said, glancing down at Arrow, who was snuggled in her lap. *At least I am from Arrow!* "I can't believe I'll be coming home soon," she said.

"I know. I'm looking forward to

when you get back, now that I'm starting to be more like my old self. I want us to spend some girl time together. That's an order!" her mom joked.

"Yes, please. I want that, too!" Charlotte said happily. "Bye, Mom. Love you." She hung up the phone. There was a big grin on her face when she turned to Arrow. "Mom sounds so much better. I think she really is going to get well again."

"That is good news," he said warmly.

Charlotte wandered out into the yard. She saw Mel on the lawn, putting Clover and Daisy into their big wire pen, so they could enjoy the fresh air and sunshine. Arrow immediately hopped over to touch noses with the gray rabbits.

Charlotte walked toward Mel. "I just spoke to Mom. She sounded much better than she did before I left. I think she's going to be fine."

A huge smile spread across Mel's face as she gave Charlotte a massive hug. "I'm so happy. Now will you promise not to keep anything like that a secret again?"

"I promise."

The two friends sat playing happily with Clover and Daisy in the sunny garden all morning. It felt just like the times they used to spend together at home.

"I thought you might like to go to the movies with just me this afternoon.

Like old times," Mel said. "There's a good comedy playing."

Charlotte thought about how much she'd wanted to spend time on her own with Mel at the beginning of the week, and about the fun she'd had at the carnival with Mel's new friends.

She smiled. "I'd love to. But maybe Jamelia and Kay could come with us?"

"Of course! I'll go and call them," Mel said.

Arrow nodded his approval as Mel ran into the house. Charlotte realized that her mom had been right. It was nice having three girlfriends instead of just one.

All of a sudden, she noticed that Arrow's key was glowing like a tiny sun. He leaped away from Clover and Daisy's pen and ran behind a huge bush toward the edge of the yard.

Charlotte knew that the moment she had been dreading was here. Her heart started pounding as she jumped up and chased after him.

At the end of the garden, she saw a cloud of shimmering crystal dust that twinkled with tiny rainbows swirling around Arrow. Suddenly, he appeared in his true form. A tiny fluffy caramel-brown-and-white bunny no longer, but a magnificent rabbit the size of a large cat. His silky pure-white fur sparkled in the sunlight and his large ears seemed to have been dipped in molten silver.

"Arrow!" Charlotte gasped. She'd almost forgotten how beautiful he was. "You're . . . you're leaving right now, aren't you?"

Jewel-bright rainbows glimmered in his wise chocolate-brown eyes.

"I must. Moonglow Meadow urgently needs more of the key's magic and the warren will be hungry."

Charlotte understood. She was tempted to beg him to stay, but knew she must be strong enough to let him go. "I'll never forget you," she whispered, her voice breaking. Bending

down she opened her arms and Arrow
came forward to let her hug him one
last time.

"I will not forget you, either. You
have been a good friend, Charlotte."

Charlotte laid her cheek against his
wonderful silky fur for a moment longer
and then Arrow moved back. "Farewell,
Charlotte. Always follow your dreams,"
he said in a velvety voice.

There was a final flash of light as crystal dust showered down around Charlotte and crackled as it hit the grass. Arrow faded and was gone.

Charlotte blinked away tears, her throat aching. She knew she was going to miss him very much. Then she noticed that something was lying on the grass. It was a single rainbow crystal drop. Wiping her eyes, Charlotte bent down and picked it up. The drop tingled against her palm as it turned into a pure white pebble in the shape of a bunny.

Charlotte slipped it into her pocket. It would be a reminder of the magic bunny and the wonderful adventure they had shared.

"Take care of Moonglow Meadow. And give my love to the other magic rabbits," she whispered under her breath.

"Charlotte!" called a familiar voice.

She looked up to see her mom walking into the garden, holding a pet carrier. Charlotte's eyes widened as she took in her mom's bright eyes and healthy pink cheeks.

"Mom! Oh, Mom!" she ran toward her, her heart almost bursting with happiness as she gave her a hug.

Her mom hugged her back. "Mel's mom invited your dad and me to come and spend a few days here. We left just after I spoke to you on the phone. She said we could bring this little guy with us. He's for you."

Charlotte looked into the pet carrier at the cute fluffy brown-and-white bunny. He had big soft brown eyes, just like Arrow, but without the rainbows.

Charlotte gazed adoringly at her new bunny. "I know just what I'm going to call him—Magic!"

About the AUTHOR

Sue Bentley's books for children often include animals, fairies, and magic. She lives in Northampton, England, in a house surrounded by a hedge so she can pretend she's in the middle of the countryside. She loves reading and going to the movies, and writes while watching the birds on the feeders outside her window and eating chocolate. Sue grew up surrounded by small animals and loved them all—especially her gentle pet rabbits whose fur smelled so sweetly of rain and grass.

Don't miss

Magic Bunny: Chocolate Wishes

Magic Bunny: Vacation Dreams

Don't miss these
Magic Puppy books!

Don't miss these
Magic Kitten books!

Magic Ponies

Don't miss these
Magic Ponies books!